Pocket Pirates

# The Great Drain Escape

2

Chris Mould

Aladdin
New York London Toronto Sydney New Delhi

This book is a work of fiction. Any references to historical events, real people, or real places are used fictitiously. Other names, characters, places, and events are products of the author's imagination, and any resemblance to actual events or places or persons, living or dead, is entirely coincidental.

ALADDIN
An imprint of Simon & Schuster Children's Publishing Division
1230 Avenue of the Americas, New York, New York 10020
First Aladdin paperback edition June 2018

Originally published in Great Britain by Hodder Children's Books
Published under license from the British publisher
Hodder & Stoughton Limited on behalf of its publishing imprint
Hodder Children's Books, a division of Hachette Children's Group
Also available in an Aladdin hardcover edition.

Cover designed by Karin Paprocki
Interior designed by Mike Rosamilia
The illustrations for this book were rendered in pen and ink.
The text of this book was set in New Century Schoolbook.
Manufactured in the United States of America 0518 OFF
2 4 6 8 10 9 7 5 3 1
Library of Congress Control Number 2017957348
ISBN 978-1-4814-9118-1 (hc)
ISBN 978-1-4814-9117-4 (pbk)
ISBN 978-1-4814-9119-8 (eBook)

For
Francesca Emily
Spalding

BUTTON
LILY
THE BASEBOARD MICE

CAPTAIN CRABSTICKS
OLD UNCLE NOGGIN
JONES
MR. DREGBY

# CONTENTS

The Old Junk Shop

At the end of the street is an old junk shop. It's gloomy and shabby and nothing ever happens there. At least, that's what most people think. . . .

Among the odds and ends and things of no use, a dusty ship in a bottle sits gathering cobwebs on a shelf. But when the world isn't watching, a tiny pirate crew comes out to explore.

And when you're smaller than a teacup, a junk shop can be a pretty dangerous place. . . .

# Nightmares

Things were not going too well for Button the ship's boy. He was trapped in sticky webbing, unable to move, and six hungry eyes, eight spindly legs, and a mouth full of spiky fangs were heading in his direction. Mr. Dregby, the house spider, had finally caught the young Pocket Pirate in his trap and it was time for dinner.

Mr. Dregby slowly lowered himself toward Button, dangling from his spider silk. He stretched out four of his eight legs, reaching for the little pirate.

Button wriggled as hard as he could, desperately trying to free himself, and then—

*THUMP!*

He fell out of his hammock and woke up.

“Sufferin’ lobster lumps,” he gasped, rubbing his eyes and getting to his feet. “That was a *horrible* dream.”

Button decided it would be a sensible idea to climb out of the ship in a bottle and take a good look around the shelf. He

needed to be sure Mr. Dregby was safely tucked away in his corner, and not on the lookout for a Pocket Pirate–size snack.

As he slipped out through the neck of the bottle and down to the wooden shelf, he was met with a lovely surprise. The sun was shining in through the window of the old junk shop. It was a beautiful day, and perfect for exploring.

There was a loud rumbling sound.

Button looked down. "Oh dear, it's my stomach again," he groaned.

Supplies were low at the moment. The poor pirate crew had barely eaten for days. They were getting by on stale bread-crumbs and a piece of moldy old cheese left over from their last adventure. And that wasn't really enough to fill the tummies of four pirates and one ship's cat.

Old Uncle Noggin and Captain Crabsticks were big eaters, and the youngest member of the crew, Lily, could pack away the grub too. Button had even tried chewing on the leaves of a potted plant, but that had left him with a terrible tummy ache.

The problem had started when the owner of the junk shop, Mr. Tooey, had moved Doyle's basket under the Pocket Pirates' shelf. The shipmates needed to find a different way down to floor level that avoided the sly, slobbery dog.

The only thing Doyle was good for was keeping the evil baseboard mice at bay. Who knows what might happen if the mice got hold of the pirates? And they

often tried! But the Pocket Pirates *had* to leave the shelf soon, or they would starve.

Button was still pondering when Lily appeared. She gave him a stern look. She could always tell when he was plotting something.

“I’d like some fresh air,” Button announced.

“Pardon?” Lily said. “I don’t think that’s a good idea. . . . Remember what happened last time you went off on your own? Your coat got caught on that picture hook and you were nearly Mr. Dregby’s dinner!”

Button wasn’t put off. “Maybe you should come with me?” he suggested. “We could go hunting outside for breakfast and be back before the Captain and Old Uncle Noggin are awake."

Lily folded her arms and gave Button an even sterner look. "Out into the street? Are you nuts? We can't even get down from the shelf now that Doyle has moved!"

"But there must be another way down, and we're sooooo *hungry*," Button said, rubbing his tummy. "You never know what we might find out there. Once, when Uncle Noggin was younger, he found a lump of fish and three fries inside an old newspaper."

Lily made a *hmph* sound and rolled her eyes.

"Did you hear me, Lily?" Button said.

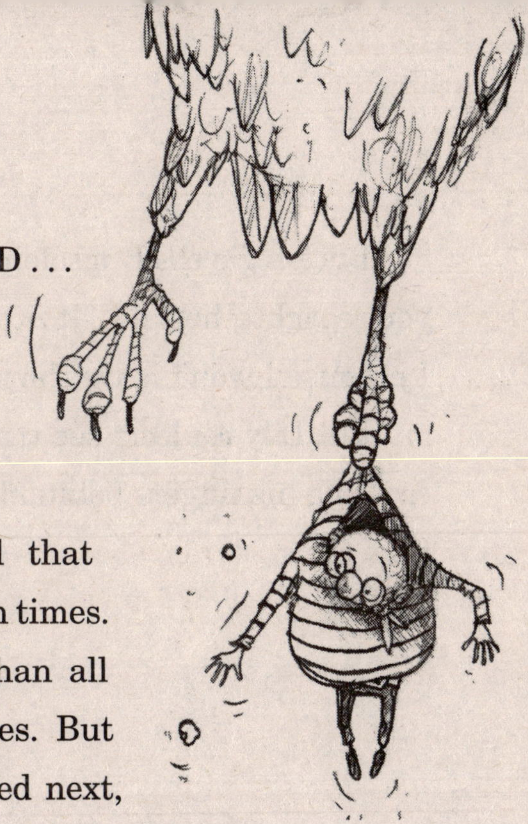

"FISH . . . AND . . . FRIES!"

"Yes, I heard you!" said Lily. "We've heard that story a million times. Even more than all his other tales. But what happened next, Button? He was attacked by a pigeon! Carried away and left up a tree. He's still got the scars to prove it. You know I like adventure as much as the next pirate, but it's too dangerous out there!"

Button gave Lily a solemn look. "Okay, you're right," he said. "It *is* too dangerous. I promise I won't leave the shelf."

But Lily couldn't see that Button was crossing his fingers behind his back.

# Down 'n' Out

As Button snuck away from the ship in a bottle later on, he wished he'd had more than a breadcrumb and a scrap of cheese for breakfast. It was quite hard to go adventuring on an empty stomach.

Ahead of him was a cable that ran all the way down the wall. If he could wrap himself around it tightly enough, he might be able to slide down to the wooden floor and land without Doyle noticing him . . .

Button took hold of the cable, then had a good look to make sure Mr. Dregby wasn't lurking. He didn't want any nasty surprises on his way down. He took a deep breath, and WHEEEEEE! He slid from the shelf, all the way to the floor.

So far, so good.

No sign of Doyle stirring. Now Button's biggest problem was getting through the front door of the shop. He looked back up at the shelf. There would be trouble if his shipmates knew he had ventured off alone, but if he could get back with supplies before they realized, he might get away with it. He was sure he would find all sorts of edible treasures out there in the big outdoors, and who was going to scold him if he brought back food?

He stared at the mailbox. Too high. He'd never reach it, let alone manage to push it open. How about the bottom keyhole? Nope. Button was small, but not small enough to squeeze through that hole.

Then he noticed a bag of trash waiting by the door. Mr. Tooey always did the trash first thing in the morning, so Button knew it would be put outside soon. He took another quick look around for any dangers, then scurried over to the bag and pulled himself up into its slippery plastic folds. He snuggled down in a battered old cookie jar and waited.

Before long, the sound of Mr. Tooey's footsteps came down the hallway. The trash bag was lifted into the air and the shop door opened with a *tinkle*. Button clung tightly to handfuls of the black plastic as Mr. Tooey dumped it on the ground with a *thud*.

The little pirate peeked out from his hiding place. The sounds were new. The air smelled different. He was outside!

“Suffering sea urchins! Where IS that work-shy cabin boy?” said Captain Crabsticks. “The deck needs sweeping and I can’t find him ANYWHERE!”

Lily could hear the Captain bellowing from below deck. “Oh, Button . . .” she muttered. “You *promised* me that you wouldn’t leave the shelf!”

“What was that, young Lily?” said Uncle Noggin, from behind her.

“Oh, um—nothing,” said Lily quickly. Luckily, before Noggin could ask any more questions, Jones, the ship’s cat, woke up and started meowing for his breakfast.

"Button! Jones wants feeding, lad! If we've got anything to feed him, that is. . . . Where are you, Button?" Uncle Noggin called as he headed out of the ship in search of the cabin boy.

It wasn't long before everyone realized Button was missing.

"Anything could have happened to him," muttered Uncle Noggin. "Once, my old aunt Maud went missing for three days. . . . Know where she was?"

"I don't know," said Lily, "but I *think* I know where Button might be."

"Stuck fast inside a cheesecake," Noggin continued, paying no attention to Lily.

"He's gone to get breakfast," Lily said.

"Dreadful time," Uncle Noggin went on. "She sank into that gloopy lemon topping so deeply, she couldn't move a muscle."

"Well, when I say *gone to get breakfast*, I mean, you know . . . he might have gone *outside* to get it. . . . "

"Good thing we found her when we did. She never ate cheesecake again. Terrible, it—Did you say OUTSIDE?" said Uncle Noggin, turning to Lily in horror.

"Looks like it," Lily said. "He was desperate to find us more food."

Noggin rubbed his tummy and pondered. "Well, he's been very foolish to go alone, but the boy's got spirit! Can't leave him out there on his own—good thing there's a secret air vent I know of that'll take us outside. Cap'n, sir, better bring your umbrella, looks like rain!"

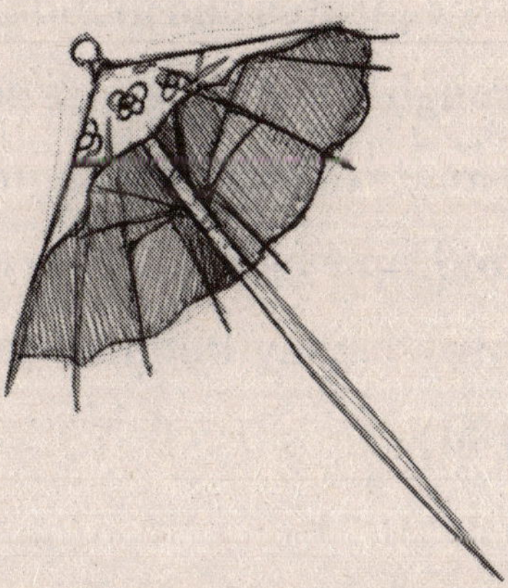

By the time the pirates had found their way outside, through Uncle Noggin's secret air vent, large splats of rain had begun to fall. A single raindrop was enough to drench a Pocket Pirate, so they huddled in a doorway to stay dry.

"What now, Captain Crabsticks?" asked Lily.

"Not sure, dear gal," the Captain replied, thoughtfully stroking his mustache. "I say, Noggin, old chap—any bright ideas?"

But Uncle Noggin was distracted.

"Look," he cried. "Over there, by those bins."

"What is it?" Lily said. "Can you see Button?"

"No. Better than that."

"Better?" said Lily in surprise.

"A bit of sandwich! I *think* I can see roasted red peppers. . . . Crew, it's our lucky day!"

“Uncle NOGGIN!” Lily scolded. “We’re supposed to be looking for Button.”

“But it’s got goat’s cheese in it too. . . .”

The rain started to bucket down.

"Stay where you—" Lily started, but it was too late. Uncle Noggin was off, dodging the falling raindrops as he zigzagged his way toward the sandwich.

Lily and Captain Crabsticks watched nervously as Noggin scooped up his prize and turned to head back to the doorway. But just as he took his first step, a sudden gush of water flowed down the pavement and knocked him clean off his feet.

Lily held her breath as Uncle Noggin disappeared beneath the water, but to her relief, it wasn't long before he bobbed back up again, still grasping his sandwich with one hand and clinging to a floating lollipop with the other. The lollipop lifeboat sailed along on the current, picking up speed as the rain got heavier and heavier.

For a short while, Uncle Noggin looked like he was enjoying the ride. But then his eyes widened as he spotted what was ahead. . . .

A drain!

“NO!” Lily yelled, and splashed into the water in Noggin’s direction, but the Captain clutched at the tails of Lily’s coat and pulled her back into the safety of the doorway.

As the pirate pair looked on in horror,

their poor shipmate disappeared down the drain and out of sight.

Meanwhile, Button was sheltering inside an old milk carton that had fallen on its side. He'd been caught in the rain before he'd had a chance to look

for food, but at least he was dry. Suddenly, something familiar rushed by on a thundering gush of water, with a yell of, "HELLLLLPPPPPPPP!"

"Blistering barnacles! It's Uncle Noggin!" Button gasped. "I'm coming, shipmate! Hold on!"

But as Button scrambled out of the milk carton, he could see that he was too late. Uncle Noggin had already disappeared into the darkness of the storm drain.

"Buuuuttttttonnnnnnnnnnnnnn!"

The ship's boy turned at the sound of his name.

For the second time that day, a familiar sight was rushing toward him on the river of rainwater. It was Captain Crabsticks and Lily, using bottletops as floats.

Captain Crabsticks stretched out his hand. "Grab a hold, young Button!" he yelled. "We're on a rescue mission!"

Button didn't have to think twice. He took a flying leap into the water, just managing to grasp the Captain's hand as he and Lily sailed by.

The drain was getting closer and closer. Button bit his lip. Other than Uncle Noggin, what might be waiting down there in the darkness?

He didn't have long to wonder. With a deafening rush of water, the three Pocket Pirates plunged into the drain.

Button lost his grip on the Captain's hand. He felt like he was falling for miles, until, with a great SPLASHHHHH, he landed in yet more water. He coughed and spluttered, shivering and trying to stay above the surface. It was pretty dark inside the drain, and chilly too. He pushed his dripping hair out of his eyes.

Lily and the Captain bobbed up next to him.

"Good thing I taught you both to swim in that goldfish bowl all those years ago," said Captain Crabsticks.

"Is that what it feels like to walk the plank?" Lily said, and coughed up a stomachful of rainwater.

"I'm so sorry," said Button, feeling ashamed. "This is all my fault. I shouldn't have left the shop."

"You're right, young chap. You *shouldn't* have left the shop," the Captain said. "But Uncle Noggin shouldn't have gone chasing after that sandwich either. Now, let's put our thinking caps on and work out how we can get back to dry land."

Just then, something moved in the water.

"What was that?" whispered Lily in alarm.

"I don't know, but I think I saw a tail. . . ." Button whispered back.

"Rats," said the Captain. "They like it down here in the drains."

"I hope they're not as evil as Pepper Jack and the other baseboard mice in the shop," Lily said, in a panicked voice. "They'll swallow us whole!"

"Look there, up ahead," Button said,

“there’s a brick sticking out of the wall. We can climb out. Maybe we’ll be able to see Uncle Noggin from there.”

The pirates swam over to the brick ledge, struggling against the swirling

current as it tried to tug them in different directions. They hauled themselves out one by one and sank into a soaking heap.

Something that wasn't a rat came bobbing past in the water.

"Ergh . . . What is THAT?" Lily said.

"Is that . . . red pepper?" said Button, peering into the murk.

"I think it's come from Uncle Noggin's sandwich," Captain Crabsticks said. "He must be nearby!"

"UNCLE NOGGGGGGGINNNN!" Button called into the darkness, his voice bouncing off the brick walls and echoing around the murky drain.

They waited and waited, holding their breath, but there was no reply.

"Sorry, crew. He's not out there," the Captain said sadly, pulling his coat more tightly around him. "And, by Neptune, we can't stay on this ledge forever, we'll freeze!"

"I wish there was something to sail on," said Lily. "The water's so cold."

And just as the words came out of her mouth, Button spotted something else floating toward them in the distance.

"It's *definitely* a rat this time," said Lily, shuddering.

"I can't see a tail, Lily," Button replied, leaning out as far as he could from the ledge to have a good look. "Actually, I think it might be a bit of wood. Hang on . . ."

"What IS that revolting smell?" Captain Crabsticks said, wafting his hat in front of his face.

There was a sudden splash as Button, who had been leaning out too far, toppled into the water. And at exactly the same time, Lily yelped.

"It's not a rat! And it's not wood, either. Button . . . I think you might want to get out of that water . . . QUICK!"

"Ahem." The Captain coughed. "It's—er—a big brown *pirate ship* . . . from the world of *lavatory*."

"A GIANT POO!" shrieked Button, and frantically swam back to the ledge.

He pulled himself out of the water just in time to avoid being bashed on the head by the floating lump.

After that, no one wanted to get into the water again. How in the Seven Seas were they going find Uncle Noggin and escape now?

The three little pirates sat on their ledge feeling very glum.

They had lost a crewmate, they were cold and hungry, and they really, really, REALLY didn't want to get back into the stinky drain water.

Suddenly, they heard a gentle splashing

sound, closely followed by a cheerful voice singing a sea shanty.

"Heave-ho, heave-ho, drop the anchor, away we go. . . ."

Button gasped. It couldn't be!

"Uncle Noggin?" he called.

"Ahoy there, me hearties!" came the reply.

Balancing on his lollipop like it was a surfboard and using a cotton swab as a paddle, Uncle Noggin steered his way over to the ledge, a huge cheesy grin on his face at the sight of his friends.

"Welcome back, old chap," the Captain said, shaking Noggin's hand.

"So glad to see you again, Uncle Noggin,"

Lily cried, forgetting how angry she'd been with him for running off after the sandwich.

She and Button both threw their arms around the soggy, stinky old pirate, giving him an enormous squeeze.

"So, now what do we do?" said Uncle Noggin, propping up his lollipop and cotton swab and settling himself down on the ledge. "We're still stuck in a drain, we're miles underground, and none of us knows how to get out again."

For what seemed like hours, the Pocket Pirates tried to plot their escape. Most of the ideas were interrupted by Uncle Noggin and his tales of adventure, not to mention food. It was as if Uncle Noggin had a recipe to go with every story, but talking about food only made the pirates feel hungrier.

They were getting nowhere fast, until Button suddenly had one of his bright ideas.

"Uncle Noggin, will you tell us your story about the gingerbread man?" he asked.

"Now now, lad," said Captain Crabsticks. "It's not really the time for tall tales of cookies."

"*Mmm.* Cookies . . ." Lily murmured.

"Ah yes, the gingerbread man," began Uncle Noggin, licking his lips and ignoring the Captain. "Poor old chap. He was baked in the oven by an old lady and when she opened the oven door, he leapt out and ran for it. The old lady chased after him but he was so fast she couldn't catch him.

And neither could anybody else. On he went, running faster and faster . . ."

"Then what?" asked Button, a bit impatiently.

"Well, he came to a river eventually. He couldn't swim, but a fox offered to carry him across."

"Thought so," said Button, grinning. "How about we ask a rat to carry *us*? They are bound to know the way to get up to the pavement."

"Button, you really *are* a clever sort of chap," the Captain said, clapping the cabin boy on the back.

"Hang on," Lily interrupted. "What about the end of the story?"

"You mean the bit where the sly old fox tossed the gingerbread man up into the air, then caught him in his mouth and ate him in one bite?" Noggin said.

"Yes . . ." Lily said, going a bit pale. "*That* bit."

"Oh, rats aren't really that sly," insisted Uncle Noggin. "There'd be no funny business like that where rats are concerned."

"But how can you be sure?" Lily asked. "I don't want to be tossed in the air, caught in a rat's mouth, and eaten in one bite, thanks very much."

"Aha," said Uncle Noggin, with a toothy grin, "then I think I may have a plan that you'll like the sound of. It's not just young Button who has the good ideas around here, y'know!"

Uncle Noggin opened the top of his bag to reveal the sandwich that had got him into trouble in the first place.

"We can use this as payment," he announced proudly. "It's a bit soggy, but it's far tastier than any of us scurvy sailors! Now, we just need a rat to come along . . ."

They didn't have long to wait before the shape of a rat appeared below. Its furry back rose slightly above the water and its tail flickered behind like a rudder.

Captain Crabsticks took out his sword and tapped it on the brick ledge, then called out to the rat, "I say, er, *Mr.* Rat, could we have your attention for

a moment? I have a suggestion that may be of interest to you."

The rat took no notice. The Captain tapped his sword again.

"Now listen here, old chap. We need to employ your services. We're in a bit of a bind and could do with getting out of this insufferable drain. We'll pay you of course, we're an honorable bunch. There's food in it for you. . . . Do you understand? Foooood."

The rat's ears pricked up. He paddled over and came to a gentle stop alongside the brick ledge, like he was a row boat in a harbor. He waited, his back hunched and out of the water.

The Captain instructed his crew to

climb aboard. Button went first, clambering on to the slippery wet fur. The tale of the gingerbread man stuck in his mind. Uncle Noggin seemed pretty sure, but what if the rat was not to be trusted? What if he got hungry halfway across and decided to eat them, like the fox in the story did?

Lily nudged Button, snapping him out of his

worries. She settled down behind him, followed by Uncle Noggin. The Captain stood at the back, as if he were steering a ship.

"Cast off!" he shouted, and the huge rodent began to paddle his way through the murky blackness.

The closer they got to the middle, the more nervous Button felt. He squeezed his eyes shut and waited to be tossed in the air and swallowed whole.

But the rat kept on paddling, and soon they were clambering off again on the other side.

Uncle Noggin lifted the soggy sandwich out of his bag and dropped it into the rat's open mouth.

With one huge gulp it was gone and then so was the rat.

"Safe sailing, old chap," said the

Captain, saluting as the rat disappeared with a small splash and a flick of his tail.

"Now, crew, let's climb up this tunnel and get back to dry land!"

“Er . . . Cap’n, sir? You might want to look up,” said Button.

Above their heads was a tunnel made of bricks, with little bits sticking out enough for the Pocket Pirates to climb on. Only problem was, the bricks were covered in slime. And the slime seemed to be moving!

“What IS that?” said Lily, shuddering.

Button bravely got closer to the pulsing blobs. He could see hairy legs and feelers and sharp pincers and prickly horns. He gulped. Cockroaches and centipedes and all manner of other insects! They were like enormous sea monsters to the little pirate.

Uncle Noggin started to shake. His eyes bulged and his knees knocked.

"Don't worry. He'll be fine," the Captain said to Lily and Button, covering up Uncle Noggin's ears as he explained. "Just a small incident with a cockroach in his younger days."

"Wonder what happened?" Lily whispered to Button.

"Don't know," Button whispered back. "But now's probably not the time to ask!"

Uncle Noggin took great wheezing breaths and wiped his forehead with his handkerchief, steadying his nerves.

"Ready to climb, old chap?" the Captain asked gently.

"Just about," Uncle Noggin replied. His knees had stopped knocking, but there was still a slight shake in his voice.

The Pocket Pirates stood beneath the slimy bricks. Captain Crabsticks drew his darning-needle sword, held it out in front of him and began to move upward. One brick at a time, he climbed up and up, giving the prickly beasties a good prod with his sword as he went. With a squeal and a squelchy scuttle, each insect darted back into its hole.

"Quick, crew! Follow me closely!" the Captain called down.

Lily and Button grabbed the bricks and started to climb after Captain Crabsticks as fast as they could. It wouldn't be long before the cockroaches would feel brave enough to come out of their holes again!

Uncle Noggin came last, climbing with his eyes shut and hanging on for dear life to the tails of Button's waistcoat.

“Are we there yet?” the old pirate called out, hopefully.

“Um, not quite yet, Uncle Noggin,” Lily replied. “You’re doing great. Keep going!”

The drains were giving off a dreadful smell.

“It smells even worse than the giant poo!” Button said, feeling a bit queasy.

On and on they climbed, hoping that they'd breathe fresh air soon.

Then Uncle Noggin gave a blood-curdling screech. "ARGGGGGHHHHH! Get it off me! Helllllppppppp!"

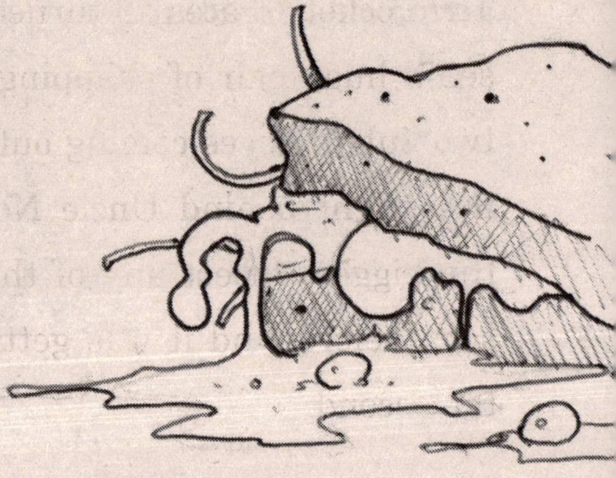

# A Beetle's Breakfast

The Pocket Pirates all turned in horror to see a huge pair of snapping pincers and two bulging eyes coming out of the darkness right behind Uncle Noggin. It was the biggest insect any of them had ever seen before, and it was getting closer by the second.

Uncle Noggin hurtled up the slippery bricks toward his crewmates, swatting away the beast's hairy feelers as best he could. But the poor pirate wasn't quick enough, and the mighty pincers snapped together on Uncle Noggin's round bottom.

"ARGGGGHHHHHHH!!!!"

"Uncle Noggin! Are you hurt?" Lily yelled to her crewmate.

"No! I'm okay! But the scoundrel's got hold of my best trousers!" Noggin yelled back. He continued to scramble up the brickwork, but there was a loud ripping sound as he left the seat of his trousers behind in the insect's pincers.

The little pirates found a ledge big

enough for them all to fit on and pulled Uncle Noggin up to safety. They formed a huddle as the beast came closer. The Captain leaned out, jabbing his sword at the insect and trying to drive it back to its hole. But this one refused to scuttle away.

Button grabbed one of the feelers and gave it a yank. Sharp pincers snapped together just above his head so he quickly let go. The crew were jabbing, yanking, and pulling at whatever they could but nothing was working. How were they going to get out of this drain without becoming a beetle's breakfast?

Then Button had another of his brilliant ideas.

“Distract it, crewmates!” he yelled. And as the Captain rapped on the beastie’s solid shell, Lily grabbed one of its spiky feelers. Uncle Noggin danced around, waving his arms to take attention away from Button, while the young cabin boy shrugged off his backpack and pulled out a matchstick.

“Oh, good thinking, Button!” Lily cried, looking over her shoulder at him. “Fire will definitely scare it off!”

But when Button scraped the matchstick along the brick to strike it alight, nothing happened. The wall was soaking wet, and now the matchstick was soggy and useless.

Button was about to throw it away in despair when Lily stopped him. "Hang on," she shouted. "I've got an even better idea!"

She let go of the insect's feeler, grabbed the matchstick from Button's hands and pushed him in front of her. Captain Crab-sticks and Uncle Noggin gasped.

"Well now, young Lily, I don't think that's quite—" the Captain began, but was cut off by a yelp from Button.

"What? Your idea is to use ME as live bait?"

"Shhhh, don't move," Lily hissed.

The gaping jaws of the insect were now close enough to swallow Button's nose. A bit of slimy goo dripped from one of its pincers and landed with a *splat* on Button's shoe.

"GARGGGHHHHHH, hurry up, Lily! Whatever it is you're going to do, get on with it before I'm mincemeat!"

In one quick movement, Lily shoved Button to the side and thrust herself forward, the matchstick clutched in her hands. The matchstick jammed in the insect's hungry jaws, sending it into a snapping tizzy. It completely forgot about the Pocket Pirates.

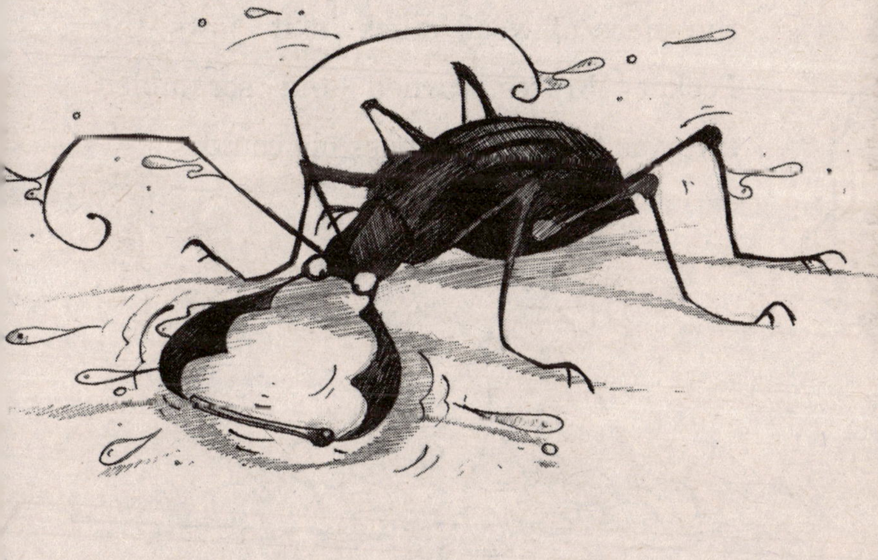

"Bravo, shipmates!" the Captain said. "Fine work."

"Thanks, Cap'n!" Lily said proudly.

"You young 'uns saved my bacon!" Uncle Noggin cheered. "Although I've still got a nasty draft around my behind . . ."

And as the beetle continued to work itself into a frenzy trying to get ahold of the piece of wood stuck in its jaws, the Pocket Pirates turned and scrambled away as fast as they possibly could.

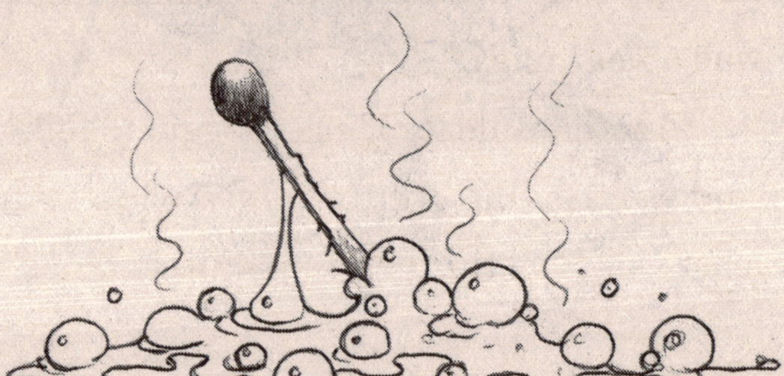

# At the Top

"Phew!" Button said, once they had got far enough away to stop for a breather. "That was a near miss."

"Another tale for Uncle Noggin to tell," said Lily, giving Button a sly wink. "At least we know this one is definitely true!"

11

The pirates were tired, soggy, and pretty stinky, but they continued to climb. They'd been stuck underground for ages and it was starting to feel like they would never reach the top.

Everyone's tummies were rumbling loudly.

"I'd do anything for fish and fries right about now," Uncle Noggin grumbled.

"Me too," Lily agreed. "Or hot chocolate. With marshmallows on top."

The Captain joined in. "I'd like some

cheese and biscuits. Or perhaps a nice slice of ham."

"Please stop talking about food!" Button begged. "My tummy is rumbling loudly enough already!"

They climbed on, trying to think of anything else but food, until to everyone's

delight, daylight could be seen above their heads. It was still far away, like a tiny pinprick in the darkness, but it meant that they were getting nearer to the pavement!

"One final push, crew. Heave-ho! Heave-ho!" the Captain said cheerily.

When the weary little pirates reached the top, they helped each other through the open grate.

They squinted in the bright sunlight and wrung out their soggy clothes the best they could.

"Ahem," said the Captain, clearing his throat. "Now that we are back on dry land, there's something I would like to say. . . . Young Button, you must remember that you are a mere cabin boy. You are NOT a hero. We are always in danger when we are inside the shop, let alone outside. And we're still not home. Who knows what perils we might encounter before we even reach the shop. We are still in terrible danger—"

"But—"

"No interrupting, Button, this is important," the Captain continued. "We could meet something out here at ANY moment that would put an end to us all."

"But there's a—"

"I must say, this is most unlike you, Button. You must listen while your captain is talking, old chap. You need to know

where the dangers are. Out here, there's trouble for a Pocket Pirate at every corner."

"But there's a—"

"Are you listening to a single word I—?"

"There's a CAT!" Button yelled. "Behind you!"

The Captain whipped around to see a huge, hairy ginger cat heading their way, licking his lips at the sight of his next meal.

"RUN, crew! Chop-chop!" Captain Crabsticks ordered.

The little pirates hurried over the bumpy pavement as fast as their legs could carry them, the huge fur ball following. However fast they ran, the cat easily followed, taking his time as he padded along menacingly behind.

They took a sharp turn down a side street, hoping to shake off the alley cat. But it was a dead end. They were trapped.

The cat rounded the corner into the side street and came toward them, its sharp teeth bared and a hungry look on its face.

This time, there would be no escape.

"I'd hoped I wouldn't have to use this again today," Captain Crabsticks sighed, drawing his sword for the second time.

Button looked inside his bag. The matchstick was gone, and all he had left was a safety pin. It wasn't much use, but he put it up in the air anyway, pretending it was

a weapon. He hoped that Lily had another brilliant plan up her sleeve, because he had truly run out of ideas. . . .

The cat was now close enough for its whiskers to tickle the little pirates. Button gulped. Its teeth looked very sharp indeed. It could probably swallow them all whole in a second.

"Lily! If you've got a plan, now might be a good time to share it!" Button yelped.

"Sorry Button, I'm all out of plans," Lily said, her fists raised in front of her.

But then the cat stopped in its tracks. It took a sniff. And another. Its nose wrinkled up and its mouth dropped open, then it turned and ran away, rounding the corner and leaving the Pocket Pirates alone in the side street.

"Ha! We must smell *really* bad." Uncle Noggin laughed.

"Thank goodness for all that stinky drain water," said Button as he shakily lowered his safety pin.

"Maybe we should have a bath in drain water every day," Lily added. "It might help us get rid of Doyle!"

A chorus of rumbling bellies started up, as if in agreement.

"Now, can we *please* find something to eat?" Button begged.

"Very well," said the Captain. "But we don't have long—it'll be dark before we know it, and we must be safely back in the junk shop before then. Hungry or not."

If there was one good thing about being outside on the street, it was the fact that there were a lot more opportunities to find food.

"You just have to look for the signs,"

said Uncle Noggin, who was now giving the others an expert lesson in searching for snacks. "Firstly, a paper bag on the

ground will, more often than not, contain some sort of delicious morsel. Take the pastry crumb as an example. A pastry crumb is the perfect Pocket Pirate–size treat—easy to carry around, tasty and filling. It's quite often topped with some kind of sauce, or, if you're lucky, a bit of meat. OR, if you're really lucky, maybe even some cheese!"

Lily and Button looked at each other, wide-eyed. Cheese was every pirate's favorite food. They'd once been on a dangerous expedition to the freezing cold place called Fridge, just to get some cheese. They were both daydreaming about that golden lump of cheesy treasure as Uncle Noggin continued with his lesson.

"Back alleys and trash cans are a must. It's an all-you-can-eat buffet for us Pocket Pirates. But where there is treasure there is also danger. Such places attract the most devilish of scurvy street lurkers. Cats and rats, and c-co-cockro . . . um, insects."

Button knew that poor Uncle Noggin couldn't even bring himself to say the word "cockroach." He wondered again what had happened to Uncle Noggin to make him so scared.

"I happen to know that Mr. Tooey keeps his trash can at the back of the shop," Captain Crabsticks announced. "I say we head there without further delay!"

So, after checking for any lurking cats or beetles—or other dangers—the Pocket Pirates ducked out of the side street and headed for the cobbled walkway that ran around the back of the old junk shop.

All they could think of was food.

# The Big Feast

The pirates waited until shoppers had passed by and the way was clear of heavy boots and spike-heeled shoes. They couldn't let themselves be seen by the big people, and they didn't want to get squished either.

They clambered over the cobblestones,

which was no easy task. Finally they found a hiding place under a large wheeled bin. From there they could peer out for things to eat, without becoming a meal themselves.

"To work, crew!" said Captain Crabsticks. "Let's fill our faces and stuff our empty tummies, then we must collect what we can to take back to the shelf. I shall stand guard over you all, if someone wouldn't mind just bringing me something to eat now and again."

Button headed straight for an empty drinks can. He poked his head inside and took a huge slurp of something that was bubbly and fizzy. It tasted delicious, especially after all the horrible drain water

he'd swallowed that day. He let out a huge *BURRRRRRRRPP.*

"Oops, pardon me," he said, holding his hand to his mouth.

Meanwhile, in his eagerness to get to the food, Uncle Noggin had collided with a broken eggshell and was now covered in slimy egg white. He'd narrowly missed falling into a rotting pepper as he slipped and slid around. But then he'd found a pizza box and had quickly forgotten about the eggy slime. Inside the box was a stray piece of pepperoni the size of Uncle Noggin's head. He settled himself down for a feast.

Lily munched on a grape and a chunk of chocolate, then she got to work, gather-

ing up what else she could. She picked up a sharp piece of eggshell and cut a slit in a soggy teabag, then she took off her pirate hat and patiently filled it with tea leaves, one handful at a time. When they got back to the ship in a bottle, she would dry them out and then, with the cake crumbs Button was now stuffing into his knapsack, they would be able to serve afternoon tea for a long while.

Lily moved on to a stuffed carrier bag, where she discovered an old shirt and a pair of shoes. She tore pieces of material from the shirt so that they could make new clothes and repair the seat of Uncle Noggin's trousers. A shoelace would be the perfect rope for Button to use when he went out climbing, so Lily pulled and tugged until it came free from the shoe. She looped it around her shoulders and climbed back out of the bag, pleased with her booty.

By now, Button had discovered a

chocolate cookie, half a sausage roll, and a whole chip in the corner of a discarded bag. He tried not to munch too much of the food he was supposed to be packing for later as he set about his task of breaking it into chunks and stuffing them into his backpack.

"Splendid work . . . splendid," said Captain Crabsticks, watching over his crewmates. Button had delivered him a selection of treats, and he was spearing and eating them with his sword while keeping a sharp eye out for danger. "You all right over there, old chap?" the Captain called to Uncle Noggin. The old pirate had moved on from his pepperoni and was now tackling a chicken wing the same size as he was.

"*Mmm.* Happiest I've been in a long while, sir," Noggin replied in a muffled voice, his mouth full of cold chicken. "Although, did I tell you about the time

I got stuck to a boiled candy? Was forced to lick myself unstuck. Was delicious . . ." And he carried on stuffing his face.

Eventually Lily and Button had gathered as much as they possibly could. Their arms, pockets, and bags were full to bursting. And so were their bellies. Everything seemed so much more cheerful now that they weren't hungry anymore.

But when the sun disappeared behind

a cloud, the pirates realized that time was ticking on, and it would start to get dark soon.

"We got out of the shop through Uncle Noggin's secret air vent," Lily said. "We should go back in the same way."

"Sounds good to me," Button said. "Let's get going, before the sun goes down."

And off the four little pirates headed, to the air vent, the junk shop, and home.

# A Giant Leap

"Now what?" said Button, scratching his head.

They had arrived at the air vent, only to find that someone had dumped a heavy box right in front of it. Try as they might, they couldn't move the box away, even with all four of them pushing.

Lily was so exhausted, she felt like crying. She flopped down on the pavement, jamming her hat full of tea leaves onto her head.

But then there was a squeal of brakes,

and the sound of an engine turning off. It was the junk shop owner, Mr. Tooey, pulling up in his van.

"Don't get upset, Lily," Button said, giving her a hand up. "Looks like we might be able to go back in the way that *I* got out!"

When Mr. Tooey left in his van, he always came back with a collection of new bits and pieces to sell in the shop. Now he was unloading the back, leaving boxes and bags by the front door while he went back to fetch more. When Mr. Tooey's back was turned, the Pocket Pirates snuck over to the collection of junk. There was one box with books inside, and the pirates knew that books would go on a shelf. Perfect!

They helped one another up the side of the box, dropping down inside before Mr. Tooey spotted them. It looked like they were going to be delivered right to their own doorstep!

"Budge up a bit, Uncle Noggin," Button said from their hiding place between copies of *Oliver Twist* and *Little Women*.

"Can't . . . tummy in the way . . . too full . . ." Uncle Noggin huffed and puffed as he tried to make a bit more room for Button.

"Shhhh!" Lily whispered. "He's coming back!"

As footsteps approached, the pirates fell silent. The box rose into the air and they were on their way.

"We're nearly home and dry, shipmates!" the Captain whispered.

"Dry sounds good to me, Cap'n," Lily whispered back. "I need to get out of these soggy clothes."

The familiar tinkle of the door chime told the pirates they were back indoors, and before long, the box was placed on the shelf.

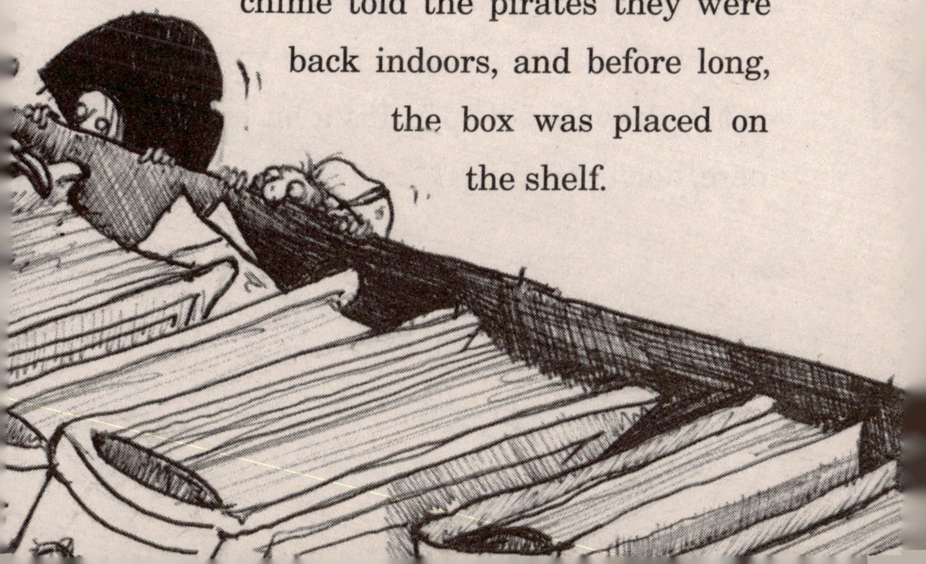

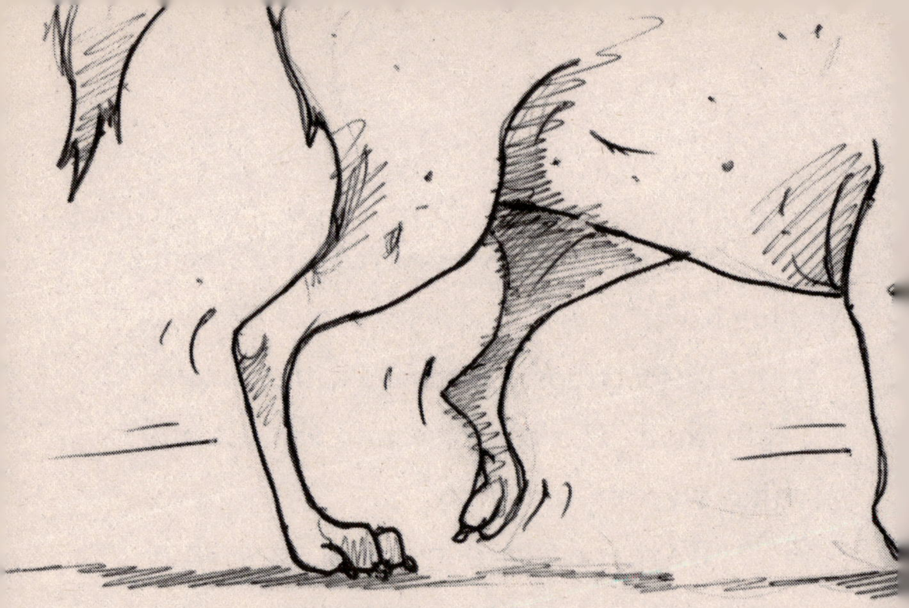

“Come on, Doyle. Heel, boy!” Mr. Tooey called to the dog as he left the room. Doyle uncurled himself from his basket and trotted after his master.

“I think I’m going to move your basket back to its old spot. It’s a bit chilly in here, don’t you think?”

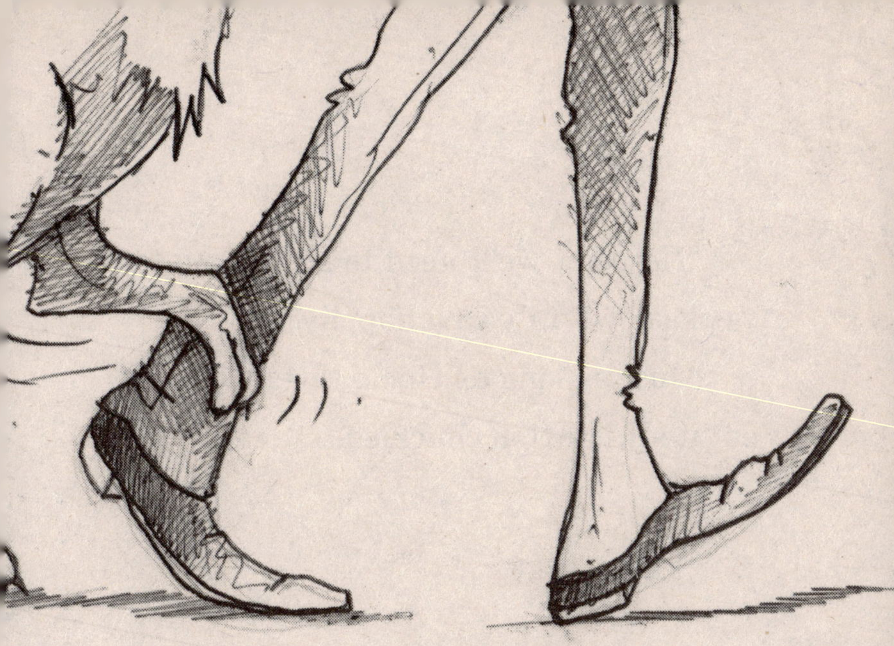

"That's enough exploring outside to last me a lifetime," Button announced, once Mr. Tooey had gone and they had clambered back out of the box and on to the shelf. "And now that the Doyle problem is solved, it won't be so difficult to find food anymore!"

“Not that we’ll need to go looking for weeks now!” Lily said happily.

“Just as long as Uncle Noggin doesn’t eat it all,” Button chuckled.

# Back on the Shelf

It wasn't long before three fresh-smelling, happy pirates were sitting by the candle stub, warming themselves by the gentle flame. Uncle Noggin was still in the bath, and the others could hear him splashing about and singing to himself. He had plenty of snacks within arm's reach.

Jones the cat had been excited to see his friends return, but refused to go anywhere near them for a cuddle or a stroke until they'd had their baths. Now he was

curled up in Lily's lap, purring and content after a huge meal of half a meatball.

Button and Lily had unpacked all the food and arranged it in the cupboard. The tastiest stuff was on high shelves, out of Uncle Noggin's reach. Now, Lily was showing Button how to mend the tear in the seat of Noggin's trousers. The cabin boy was bent over the needle and thread, concentrating hard.

Apart from Uncle Noggin's singing, all was peaceful. Just how the Pocket Pirates liked it. It had been a long and tiring day.

"Crew, I shall be happy to stay on dry land for a while," Captain Crabsticks announced. He was sitting between the pages of a book on growing your own vegetables. “Even a pirate captain can get a bit tired of water now and again.”

“I—” Lily began, but she was cut off by a crash and a sudden whooshing sound.

"Flood alerrrrrrtttttt!" Uncle Noggin yelled, tumbling along the shelf toward them, on a tidal wave of bath water.

"So much for dry land, eh, Captain?" Button said, leaping up to avoid getting totally drenched.

Noggin came to a skidding halt in front of them, coughing up soap bubbles.

"I reached for a snack and the whole sufferin' bathtub capsized," he choked, as Lily tipped water out of her boots and Jones swatted at the bubbles flying about the shelf.

“Better fetch a mop, young Button,” Captain Crabsticks said, with a chuckle.

Later that evening, when the bathtub was back upright and everything was dry again, the Pocket Pirates sat down for a bedtime snack of hot chocolate and cookie crumbs.

“Maybe we should go to sleep now, before anything else goes wrong,” Captain Crabsticks suggested, when they’d munched the last crumb and slurped the final drop of hot chocolate.

And so the little pirates blew out the candle, took down the pirate flag, and said good night.

“What shall we do tomorrow?” Button said to Lily, once they were comfortably curled up in their hammocks below deck.

“I need a rest!” Lily replied. “How about we do absolutely nothing?”

But before Button could answer, he was fast asleep, already lost in dreams of new adventures.

REAR HALLWAY
BACK DOOR
HALLWAY
STORE-ROOM
SITTING ROOM
HALL
BOOK-SHELF
Mice
N
W
E
S
The Old JUNKSHOP

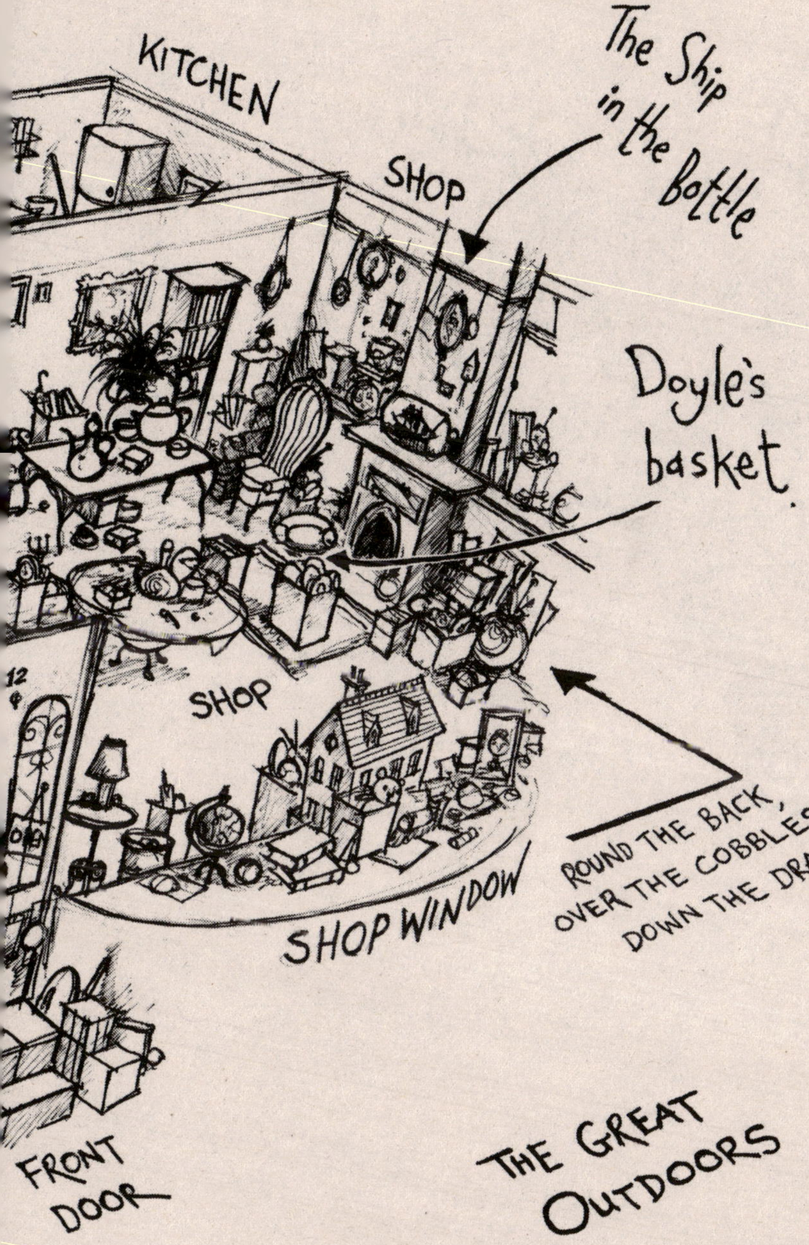
KITCHEN
The Ship in the Bottle
SHOP
Doyle's basket.
SHOP
ROUND THE BACK, OVER THE COBBLES, DOWN THE DRAIN
SHOP WINDOW
FRONT DOOR
THE GREAT OUTDOORS

Turn the page for a peek at Book 1
in the Pocket Pirates adventures:

# THE GREAT CHEESE ROBBERY

Button the ship's boy had spent most of the afternoon exploring. He'd climbed in and out of piles of books and boxes of this and that to see what he might find. He'd even snatched a quick nap inside the old cuckoo clock.

But on his way back down to the shelf, Button had caught the back of his jacket on an old picture hook and now he was hanging helplessly on the wall.

"Oh, crumbs, not again," he said out loud to himself.

He looked over the shop. It was one of those perfect evenings. The moonlight was pouring in through the window and shone a silvery blue over the ship in the bottle. Everything had been calm until now. He tried to shake himself free, but it was no good.

High above Button, something had awakened in the dark. Mr. Dregby, the house spider, was keen to make a snack out of Button. He'd had his six eyes on the boy for some time. And now he could see that his perfect meal was hanging there beneath him, waiting.

"The young ones are the juiciest," Mr. Dregby cackled in delight.

Button heard a scritching sound above and he looked up in alarm. A tangle of long hairy legs and beady eyes was rushing toward him.

And then, all at once, he felt himself being pulled by the legs. He slipped clean out of his jacket and landed in a heap on

the floor, on top of his rescuer. She let out a muffled "YELP."

It was his best friend, Lily, the youngest of the pirate crew. She jumped to her feet, waving a long darning needle in Mr. Dregby's direction. The spider scuttled grumpily back into the darkness above the shelf.

"Thanks!" said Button as he straightened himself out. "That was close."

He looked up to see his coat was still hanging on the hook.

"You're not supposed to go wandering off on your own," Lily said. "It's dangerous!'

"I was looking for an adventure," Button replied.